Most Va PUPPY

BY CAROL KIM
ILLUSTRATED BY FELIA HANAKATA

JOLLY
FISH
PRESS

Mendota Heights, Minnesota

Book design by Jake Nordby
Illustrations by Felia Hanakata

Published in the United States by Jolly Fish Press, an imprint of North Star Editions, Inc.

First Edition
First Printing, 2019

This is a work of fiction. Names, characters, places, and incidents are either the product of the author's imagination or are used fictitiously, and any resemblance to actual persons living or dead, business establishments, events, or locales is entirely coincidental.

Library of Congress Cataloging-in-Publication Data
Names: Kim, Carol, author. | Hanakata, Felia, illustrator.
Title: Most valuable puppy / by Carol Kim ; illustrated by Felia Hanakata.
Description: Mendota Heights, MN : Published in the United States by Jolly
  Fish Press, an imprint of North Star, 2020. | Series: Doggie daycare |
  Summary: "Shawn and Kat Choi must find a way to keep an energetic Jack
  Russell terrier calm before he's the first, and last, Doggie Daycare
  customer"– Provided by publisher.
Identifiers: LCCN 2019006808 (print) | LCCN 2019019198 (ebook) | ISBN
  9781631633416 (ebook) | ISBN 9781631633409 (pbk.) | ISBN 9781631633393
  (hardcover)
Subjects: | CYAC: Jack Russell terrier—Fiction. | Dogs—Fiction. | Dog day
  care—Fiction. | Moneymaking projects—Fiction. | Brothers and
  sisters—Fiction. | Korean Americans—Fiction.
Classification: LCC PZ7.1.K554 (ebook) | LCC PZ7.1.K554 Mo 2020 (print) | DDC
  [Fic]—dc23
LC record available at https://lccn.loc.gov/2019006808

Jolly Fish Press
North Star Editions, Inc.
2297 Waters Drive
Mendota Heights, MN 55120
www.jollyfishpress.com

Printed in the United States of America

TABLE OF CONTENTS

CHAPTER 1

Bouncer

"How about a kimchi stand?" asked Shawn. He popped a piece of the spicy pickled cabbage into his mouth. "You know, like a lemonade stand."

Kat, his younger sister, made a face. "Blech!" she said. "No one likes kimchi."

"Try telling that to the 50 million Korean people who eat it every day," Shawn shot back.

"We need to think of a super fabulous summer project idea before school gets out. Not a smelly one," Kat said.

"Let's go to the park," Shawn said. "I think better outside."

The San Francisco morning fog hovered around them as they left their house. A car drove past, then stopped.

"Shawn! Kat! Come meet Bouncer!" their friend Mitchell called from the car window.

The two ran up and looked in. Mitchell's sister Sasha sat next to him with a small dog in her lap. It had short white fur with black and tan patches.

"Arf! Arf! Arf arf arf arf arf!" barked the dog.

Shawn quickly backed away.

Kat leaned in and slowly reached out a hand. "Hello, Bouncer," she said. The dog licked her. Kat giggled.

"Can Sasha and I walk the rest of the way home?" asked Mitchell.

"Sure," said his father, Mr. Warren. Sasha opened the car door.

A brown and white blur shot out of the car.

"Bouncer!" Sasha screamed.

The little dog raced down the street. Shawn chased after him. The other kids followed.

Bouncer ran into the park.

Two older boys were playing catch with a Frisbee. One boy sent it sailing through the air. Bouncer leapt up.

He caught the Frisbee in his mouth.

"Whoa!" yelled the boy.

"Gotcha!" cried Shawn, grabbing Bouncer.

Sasha ran up and attached Bouncer's leash.

"Arf! Arf! Arf!" Bouncer barked, running in circles.

Mr. Warren watched from the car, frowning.

Uh oh, thought Shawn.

CHAPTER 2

A New Business

"How's it going with Bouncer?" Shawn asked Mitchell. It was two weeks later, and they were walking to school along with Kat and Sasha. "Has he chewed up any more shoes?"

Mitchell sighed. "Yesterday it was my baseball cleats and my mom's slippers. And no one can find matching socks anymore. He always chews up just one!"

"Last night Bouncer jumped onto the dining table," Sasha said. "And he ate the roast chicken mom had made for dinner."

"Yikes," said Shawn.

"Then our parents told us we are going to Seattle next weekend," said Mitchell.

"And that we may not be able to keep Bouncer if he doesn't behave!" Sasha said, tears filling her eyes.

"Oh, no!" Kat gasped.

"Maybe we can help," said Shawn.

At dinner that night, Kat said, "I still think turning the backyard into a chicken farm is a great idea. We would have fresh eggs every day!"

"Fresh chicken poop is more like it," their grandmother said.

"Don't worry, Halmoni. We have a better idea. We want to start a doggie daycare business!" Shawn said. "With Bouncer as our first customer!"

"Sasha and Mitchell's parents loved the idea," Kat said. "They wanted to know how soon we could start!"

"Is Bouncer a good dog?" Ms. Choi asked.

"Oh yes! He's very good at retrieving toys," Kat said to her mom. She knew Bouncer needed to work on following commands, but at least she was telling the truth.

"Well . . . we guess you can give it a try," their dad said.

"Yes!" Shawn and Kat said.

But Shawn was worried. Would their house survive a long weekend with Bouncer?

CHAPTER 3

First Customer

"I never knew the library had so many books about dogs," said Shawn. He and Kat were at the library doing research.

"It says Jack Russell terriers need lots and lots of exercise," Shawn said.

"I used to have a Jack Russell when I was a boy," the librarian, Mr. Perez, said. "He could jump over our fence. And it was four feet high!"

"Wow!" said Kat.

Mr. Perez smiled. "He was also the smartest dog I ever knew. He learned to bring in the newspaper, put away his toys, and run through an obstacle course."

"We need to train our friends' dog so he's better behaved," said Shawn. "Otherwise they may not be able to keep him!"

"They learn fast with the right reward," Mr. Perez said. "For a biscuit, my dog would do just about anything!"

The next day, Shawn lay on the living room floor. "I don't think I could throw another ball," he said.

"I can't believe we played fetch for an hour," Kat said, petting Bouncer.

"And that was after we had taken him to the dog park!" Shawn said.

"Maybe this wasn't such a good idea. How are we going to keep this up for two more days?" Kat moaned.

Their grandmother appeared in the kitchen doorway.

"Hi, Halmoni," called Kat.

"Time to help with the kimchi!" she said.

In the kitchen, there was a huge bowl of cabbage on the table. Halmoni added lots of red pepper and garlic. "Okay, mix it up!" she said.

Bouncer trotted into the room, nose sniffing.

The kimchi filled four jars. Kat ran to the sink. "My hands are going to smell like kimchi for a week!" she said.

"Aieeee!" their grandmother suddenly cried.

Bouncer was on the table, sniffing the bowl.

"Bouncer! No!" Shawn yelled.

The dog jumped down, knocking the bowl to the ground. Bits of kimchi went flying.

Kat tried to grab Bouncer, but he darted away. Suddenly, nose to the ground, he stopped. Then he began licking and chewing something off the floor.

"He's eating kimchi!" Kat cried.

"Time for Bouncer to go outside!" Halmoni yelled.

CHAPTER 4

Ball Dog

The next day, Shawn and Kat walked slowly to the park. Bouncer walked ahead on his leash. They passed a group of boys playing baseball. A pitcher threw the ball.

Thwack!

The batter swung, hitting the baseball over the outfielders' heads. Bouncer took off, pulling the leash from Kat's hand.

"Bouncer!" she yelled.

The dog raced to the ball, cutting in front of the outfielder. "Get that dog off the field!" he yelled.

Bouncer grabbed the ball in his mouth. He ran back to Shawn and Kat and dropped it at their feet.

"Sorry," called Shawn, throwing the ball to the pitcher.

"We better get him away from here," Kat said.

They walked to the playground. Two small girls walked up to them. "Can we pet him?" asked one.

"Sure," Kat said.

"Does he like to play fetch?" asked the other girl.

"That's one of his favorite things to do," Kat said.

Kat watched two women playing tennis nearby. One of the players served the ball. "Oops!" she yelled as the ball went out of bounds.

"Hey!" Kat cried, losing her grip on the leash. Bouncer raced toward the tennis court.

Bouncer grabbed the ball and trotted up to them, tail wagging.

"He's like a ball boy!" said the tennis player.

"A ball dog!" Kat laughed, petting

Bouncer.

On the way home, Shawn and Kat passed the soccer fields. A group of kids were playing a game. One of them kicked the ball out of play. It rolled toward Shawn and Kat.

"Here you go," Shawn said, kicking it back toward them.

"Arf! Arf!" Bouncer raced after the ball.

"Not again!" Kat cried, as the leash was pulled from her hand.

Bouncer ran up to the ball. He tried to bite it. But the ball was too big for the little dog. It shot away from him.

"Arf! Arf!"

Bouncer reached the ball and pushed it forward with his nose.

"He's dribbling the ball!" Shawn cried.

The dog dodged and weaved, keeping the ball from the players. Up and down the field he ran.

Suddenly, he stopped.

Panting, Bouncer lay down on the field. Kat ran over and picked him up. Soccer players gathered around.

"That was amazing!" a player said.

"What's his name? Messi?" another player asked, naming a famous soccer player.

Everyone laughed.

"I'll tell you what's amazing," Shawn said to Kat. "Bouncer's actually tired!"

That gave Kat an idea. That night she worked with Bouncer on his soccer skills. Shawn and Kat spent most of the next day practicing too.

The siblings couldn't wait to share their plan for Bouncer with Sasha and Mitchell.

CHAPTER 5

Most Valuable Puppy

Kat watched as her teammate dribbled the ball quickly toward the goal. Time was running out, but they had a chance to score and win the game.

"Sasha, get ready!" Kat called. Sasha ran toward her teammate.

Okay, Kat thought. *Almost . . . almost . . .*

"Bouncer!" Kat yelled suddenly. "Halt!"

The little dog suddenly stopped, the ball rolling a few inches away from him. Sasha ran up and kicked the ball hard.

POW!

The ball flew past the goalie into the net.

GOAL!

Kat ran toward Bouncer. "Good dog!" She said, pulling a treat from a pouch. Bouncer gobbled up the kimchi eagerly.

A whistle blew. The game was over. They had won!

Kat and Sasha hugged, surrounded by their cheering teammates.

"Bouncer is a changed dog," Mr. Warren said later to Kat and Shawn. "He's so well-behaved now!"

"The key is giving him a job and keeping him active," said Shawn. "And kimchi. He'll do anything for kimchi!"

"Tomorrow Bouncer works as a ball dog at our batting practice," said Mitchell.

"And the next day he's working at the tennis courts," said Sasha.

"Don't forget about soccer practice on Thursday," said Kat.

Just then, the soccer coaches walked up.

"Congratulations on your first win of the season!" said Coach Gabriella. "To mark the occasion, we would like to present a special award."

"Today's Most Valuable Player award goes to . . . Bouncer!" said Coach Erin.

"Hooray!" everyone yelled.

Kat lifted Bouncer up. "To the most valuable puppy!" she cheered.

Everyone agreed.

THINK ABOUT IT

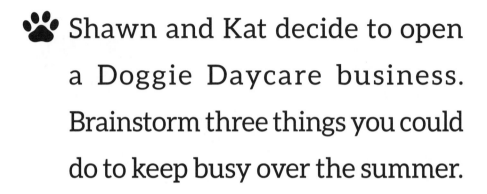 Shawn and Kat decide to open a Doggie Daycare business. Brainstorm three things you could do to keep busy over the summer.

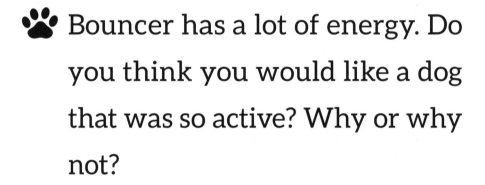 Bouncer has a lot of energy. Do you think you would like a dog that was so active? Why or why not?

 Shawn and Kat discovered that Bouncer loved kimchi. Make a list of three of your favorite foods.

ABOUT THE AUTHOR

Carol Kim lives in Texas with her husband, two daughters, and one very well-behaved dog. Her childhood was spent in Southern California, where she grew up eating kimchi every day. She writes both fiction and nonfiction for children. When she's not writing, she enjoys reading, cooking, traveling, and exploring food from different cultures.

ABOUT THE ILLUSTRATOR

Felia Hanakata is an Indonesia-based illustrator. She went to the Academy of Art University and completed her BFA in Illustration in spring 2017. She thinks storytelling breathes life and colors into the world. When she is not drawing, she usually reads, drinks lots of coffee, plays video games, or looks for inspiration in nature and her surroundings.